# BEAR PARTY

*by*
WILLIAM PÈNE DU BOIS

PUFFIN BOOKS

PUFFIN BOOKS

Viking Penguin Inc., 40 West 23rd Street, New York, New York 10010, U.S.A.
Penguin Books Ltd., 27 Wrights Lane, London W8 5TZ (Publishing & Editorial) and
Harmondsworth, Middlesex, England (Distribution & Warehouse)
Penguin Books Australia Ltd, Ringwood, Victoria, Australia
Penguin Books Canada Limited, 2801 John Street, Markham, Ontario, Canada L3R 1B4
Penguin Books (N.Z.) Ltd, 182–190 Wairau Road, Auckland 10, New Zealand

First published by The Viking Press, Inc., 1951
Viking Seafarer Edition published 1969
Published in Picture Puffins 1987

Printed in the United States of America
Set in Weiss

ISBN 0-14-050793-0

William Pène du Bois

There's a park down in
Australia named Koala Park
where real teddy bears live
in trees.

They are most always happy

and play together all day, but:

Once upon a time they became

angry with each other, no bear

remembers why, and they became

angrier and angrier.

First they stopped speaking to

each other, and then they even

stopped looking at each other and

just stared straight ahead and made

growling noises.

The wise old bear who lived at the top of the tallest Eucalyptus tree thought this behavior was TERRIBLE.

"Something must be done RIGHT AWAY!" he said to himself. He scratched his head and shouted:

"I'll give a costume ball

and all bears will be invited.

"They will all wear masks

so they won't have to tell each

other who they are.

"In this way they will soon

get together again.

"At sundown, I'll tell them

to take off their costumes and masks, and by then they'll be friends and all will once more be well in Koala Park."

The angry bears loved this idea. Each chose a different costume. There was an American

Indian Bear

a Sleeping Bear

15

a Spanish Bear

and a Clown Bear

16

a French Bear

an Angel Bear

a Nurse Bear

and a

Bullfighter Bear

There was a

Hunting Bear

a Chinese Bear

a Knight Bear

a Dancing Bear

20

a Turkish Bear

and a Napoleon Bear.

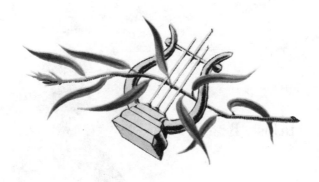

The music for the dancing was love-ly. There was an accordion that went SQUEAK SQUNK,

a triangle that went TING TING,

a guitar that went PLINK PLUNK,

and a big horn that went POOMPF POOMPF. It was a WONDERFUL party!

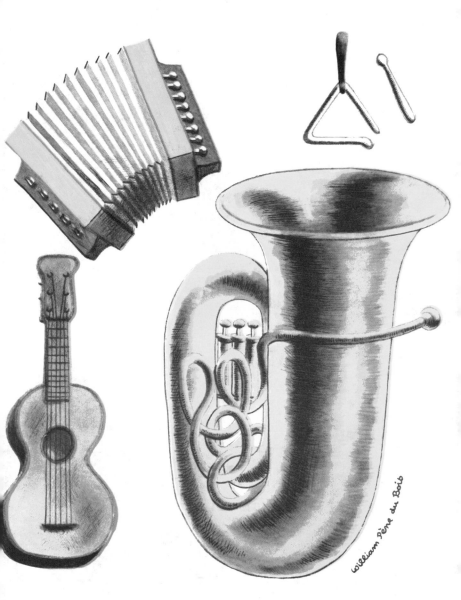

23

They did all kinds of dances.

There were Rhumbas, Sambas,

Bunny Hugs and Turkey Trots.

They also did very hard-to-do

dances which they made up all by themselves.

At sundown, the wise old bear who lived at the top of the tallest Eucalyptus tree shouted:

"OFF WITH YOUR COSTUMES AND OFF WITH YOUR MASKS!"

# The bears took off their costumes

and threw them in a big pile in the

middle of the dance floor.

They next took off their
masks and hung them on the
branch of a tree.

They turned and looked at

each other, and then something AWFUL happened. Koala bears are famous for looking very much alike, and these bears had been unfriendly for so long they could no longer tell each other apart.

The Clown Bear

didn't know the Dancing Bear.

The Hunting Bear

didn't know the Nurse Bear.

The Indian Bear didn't
know the Chinese Bear.

They started to get angry all
over again and some low growling
was heard.

The wise old bear who lived at the top of the tallest Eucalyptus tree thought this behavior was TERRIBLE.

"Something must be done RIGHT AWAY!" he said to himself. He scratched his head and thought:

"JUMP INTO YOUR COSTUMES

AND ON WITH THE DANCE!"

The bears put their costumes back on and tied on their masks and the growling noises stopped as they happily danced together far into the night.

The bears had had such a good time at the party that next day they all decided to wear a part of their costumes as a souvenir.

This was a perfect idea. With these souvenirs they could easily tell each other apart.

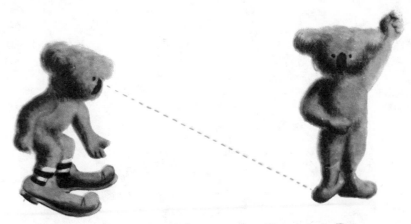

The Clown Bear knew the Dancing Bear.

The Hunting Bear knew the Nurse Bear.

The Indian Bear knew the Chinese
Bear. They all got together and
talked about what a wonderful party
it had been.

After a while they found that
they could once again tell each
other apart as just plain bears

and after that all was well once
more in Koala Park.

The wise old bear who lived at

the top of the tallest Eucalyptus tree thought this behavior was WONDERFUL. He scratched his head and thought: "From now on, in Koala Park, there must be many, many more BEAR PARTIES!"

THE
END